The Town-Musicians of Bremen

First published in English in 1993 by Floris Books
15 Harrison Gardens, Edinburgh
© Christofoor Publishers, Zeist 1992
The translation is from *The Complete Grimm's Fairy Tales*
(1978) by permission of Routledge & Kegan Paul
This version © Floris Books 1993
British Library CIP Data available
ISBN 0-86315-159-0   Printed in Belgium

The Town-Musicians of Bremen

A Grimm's fairy tale illustrated by Carla Grillis

Floris Books

A certain man had a donkey, which had carried
the corn-sacks to the mill indefatigably for many
a long year; but his strength was going, and he
was growing more and more unfit for work.
Then his master began to consider how he
might best save his keep; but the donkey,
seeing that no good wind was blowing, ran
away and set out on the road to Bremen.

"There," he thought, "I can surely be a
town-musician."

When he had walked some distance, he found a
hound lying on the road, gasping like one who had
run till he was tired.

"What are you gasping so for, you big fellow?"
asked the donkey.

"Ah," replied the hound, "as I am old and daily
grow weaker, and no longer can hunt, my master
wanted to kill me, so I took to flight. But now how
am I to earn my bread?"

"I tell you what," said the donkey, "I am going to
Bremen, and shall be town-musician there. Go with
me and engage yourself also as a musician. I will play
the lute, and you shall beat the kettledrum."

The hound agreed, and on they went.

Before long they came to a cat, sitting on the path, with a face like three rainy days!

"Now then, old shaver, what has gone askew with you?" asked the donkey.

"Who can be merry when his neck is in danger?" answered the cat. "Because I am now getting old, and my teeth are worn to stumps, and I prefer to sit by the fire and spin, rather than hunt about after mice, my mistress wanted to drown me, so I ran away. But now good advice is scarce. Where am I to go?"

"Go with us to Bremen. You understand night-music, so you can be a town-musician."

The cat thought well of it, and went with them.

After this the three fugitives came to a farmyard, where the cock was sitting upon the gate, crowing with all his might.

"Your crowing goes through and through one," said the donkey. "What is the matter?"

"I have been foretelling fine weather, because it is the day on which Our Lady washes the Christ-child's little shirts, and wants to dry them," said the cock. "But guests are coming for Sunday, so the housewife has no pity, and has told the cook that she intends to eat me in the soup tomorrow, and this evening I am to have my head cut off. Now I am crowing at the top of my lungs while still I can."

"Ah, but red-comb," said the donkey, "you had better come away with us. We are going to Bremen. You can find something better than death everywhere. You have a good voice, and if we make music together it must have some quality!" The cock agreed to this plan, and all four went on together.

They could not reach the city of Bremen in one day, however, and in the evening they came to a forest where they meant to pass the night. The donkey and the hound laid themselves down under a large tree, the cat and the cock settled themselves in the branches; but the cock flew right to the top, where he was most safe. Before he went to sleep he looked round on all four sides, and thought he saw in the distance a little spark burning; so he called out to his companions that there must be a house not far off, for he saw a light.

The donkey said: "If so, we had better get up and go on, for the shelter here is bad."

The hound thought too that a few bones with some meat on would do him good!

So they made their way to the place where the light was, and soon saw it shine brighter and grow larger, until they came to a well-lighted robbers' house. The donkey, as the biggest, went to the window and looked in.

"What do you see, my grey-horse?" asked the cock.

"What do I see?" answered the donkey. "A table covered with good things to eat and drink, and robbers sitting at it enjoying themselves."

"That would be the sort of thing for us," said the cock.

"Yes, yes! Ah, if only we were there!" said the donkey.

Then the animals took counsel together how they should manage to drive away the robbers, and at last they thought of a plan. The donkey was to place himself with his forefeet upon the window-ledge, the hound was to jump on the donkey's back, the cat was to climb upon the dog, and lastly the cock was to fly up and perch upon the head of the cat.

When this was done, at a given signal, they began to perform their music together: the donkey brayed, the hound barked, the cat mewed, and the cock crowed; then they burst through the window into the room, shattering the glass! At this horrible din, the robbers sprang up, thinking no otherwise than that a ghost had come in, and fled in a great fright out into the forest.

The four companions now sat down at the table, well content with what was left, and ate as if they were going to fast for a month.

As soon as the four minstrels had done, they put out the light, and each sought for himself a sleeping-place according to his nature and to what suited him. The donkey laid himself down upon some straw in the yard, the hound behind the door, the cat upon the hearth near the warm ashes, and the cock perched himself upon a beam of the roof; and being tired from their long walk, they soon went to sleep.

When it was past midnight, and the robbers saw from afar that the light was no longer burning in their house, and all appeared quiet, the captain said: "We ought not to have let ourselves be frightened out of our wits," and ordered one of them to go and examine the house.

The messenger finding all still, went into the kitchen to light a candle, and, taking the glistening fiery eyes of the cat for live coals, he held a lucifer-match to them to light it. But the cat did not understand the joke, and flew in his face, spitting and scratching. He was dreadfully frightened, and ran to the back-door, but the dog, who lay there, sprang up and bit his leg; and as he ran across the yard by the dunghill, the donkey gave him a smart kick with its hind foot.

The cock, too, who had been awakened by the noise, and had become lively, cried down from the beam: "Cock-a-doodle doo!"

Then the robber ran back as fast as he could to his captain, and said: "Ah, there is a horrible witch sitting in the house, who spat on me and scratched my face with her long claws. And by the door stands a man with a knife, who stabbed me in the leg. And in the yard there lies a black monster, who beat me with a wooden club. And above, upon the roof, sits the judge, who called out, 'Bring the rogue here to me!' so I got away as well as I could."

After this the robbers never again dared enter the house; but it suited the four musicians of Bremen so well that they did not care to leave it any more. And the mouth of him who last told this story is still warm.